DIARY OF A MINECRAFT ZOMBIE

BOOK 8

BACK TO SCARE SCHOOL

DIARY OF A MINECRAFT ZOMBIE

ZOMBIE

BOOK 8

BACK TO SCARE SCHOOL

BY

Zack Zombie

4

☀ SUNDAY ☀

One more week and I'm going back to school.

I can't believe I'm actually looking forward to going back to Scare School.

Don't get me wrong, I had a great summer. Even though I didn't play as much video games or eat as much CAKE as I wanted to—it was still awesome.

But I'm really looking forward to seeing all my friends at Scare School.

I'm really excited to see my ghoulfriend Sally. I haven't seen her all summer because she was touring all the Biomes with her parents.

I guess it's really good to be a Zombie and **HAVE MONEY.** You can do cool stuff like that.

But I really miss her.

Sally is the best. What I really like most about Sally is that she likes me for who I am inside. Even though sometimes my insides are hanging out on the outside.

But Sally really likes me, even though I can be a bit weird sometimes.

You see, being a 12 year old Zombie can be awkward. Especially going through puberty.

Like, lately my voice has gotten a little hoarse.

No, really. I think a horse fly laid some eggs in my throat when I was sleeping one day.

All I know is that when I'm talking, I feel something **WIGGLING** around in my throat.

Makes my voice sound really weird.

Dad says that puberty happens pretty fast for Zombies. Like one day I went from having no mold on my face to having half my face covered in different colored mold.

My Mom took a video to show how quickly the mold grew and changed color.

Right now it's a deep purple, which I think means I'm deep in thought.

It changes color a lot based on how I'm feeling.

It's kind of like a mood ring but all over my face.

Also, I started getting taller. Well, one side of me anyway.

You see one of my legs grew really long one night. It's about four inches taller than my other one. So it makes it easy to walk like a **REAL ZOMBIE** now. Before, when my legs were the same size, I walked too much like Steve and people would look at me funny.

But, I'm really glad I'm growing because now the other Mob kids at school will stop calling me names.

Being short *and a* seventh grader is not a good combination in **MOB MIDDLE SCHOOL.** All of the eighth grade kids pick on you and call you names like::

- Tiny Tim
- Short Stuff
- Mini Me
- Mini You
- Mini Zombie
- Baby Zombie
- Baby Zeke
- Runt
- Smalls

- ⊠ Squirt
- ⊠ Shortcake
- ⊠ Small Fry
- ⊠ Munchkin
- ⊠ Munch-skin
- ⊠ Shorty
- ⊠ Captain Mini Pants
- ⊠ And Captain Mini Zombie Pants

But this year I'm going to be an eighth grader and I'm going to be a lot taller. So, I should probably brush up on my name calling.

But you know, lately every time I think about being an eighth grader I get really scared. I mean, I've never been an eighth grader before. What am I supposed to do? How's an eighth grader **SUPPOSED TO ACT?**

What if the other eighth graders don't like me? Or what if the eighth grade work is too hard and I flunk out? Or what if I get a really mean Scare Class teacher? Or what if we get new bullies that transfer to the school?

You know, I think I changed my mind. I don't think I want to go to eighth grade anymore.

Man, being a Zombie in Middle School is really hard...

MNDAY

Today we went shopping for new school clothes.

Except this time my Mom and Dad told me to pick out **WHATEVER CLOTHES** I wanted. They said since I'm in eighth grade, I'm a big Zombie now.

When we got to the Zombie Mall, my Dad gave me his Zombie Credit Card.

"Spend as much as you want," my Dad said.

Did he just say what I think he said?

I had to ask him again, "As much as I want?"

"Yes, son. You're in eighth grade now. You worked really hard. You deserve it."

I couldn't believe it!

Wow, being an eighth grader comes with a lot of perks! It's like I'm entering a **WHOLE NEW WORLD.**

Who knew that eighth graders had it so good?

So, I went straight to Old Scary Navy. That's where all the cool kids go to get their clothes.

I got every shirt and every pair of pants I could find that looked cool. My shopping cart was so full I had to get another one.

I was thinking about how cool I was going to look on the first day of school.

I'm finally going to be the coolest dressed kid in school, I thought. *No*

more turquoise T-shirts and blue
pants.

When I got to the
counter, the Zombie
lady's eye sockets
got really big.

"Are all of these
for you?" she
asked. "They're
not even the same
size."

All I could say was, "Gimme, gimme,
gimme, gimme..."

After she totaled everything up, I
pulled out my Zombie Credit Card, and
I handed it to her like I had used it
for years.

She swiped the card and the register made a buzzing noise. Then she swiped it a few more times and the same thing happened. After about 10 more swipes, she picked up the phone and called the number on the card.

When she hung up, she looked at me like I was some sort of criminal.

"What are you trying to pull over on me?" she said. "This card has a limit of only $30.⁰⁰

Then she shoved all of the clothes behind the counter and set aside the only thing I could afford...

...A turquoise T-shirt and a blue pair of pants.

TUESDAY

Today we got our new school schedules in the mail.

When I looked at my new schedule I was really excited because I'm taking SCARE CLASS 201 this year.

It's a little bit more advanced than Scare Class 101. This time we're not just scaring villagers—we're scaring miners!

We only talked about scaring miners a little last year. But this year we're actually going to go out and do it.

I can't wait because miners drop the coolest stuff, like red-stones, gold, diamonds and emeralds!

I don't really need that stuff. But if I give it to Steve, he can trade it with some villagers for some **EXTRA PIECES** of cake.

I heard that one emerald can probably get me like a thousand pieces of cake.

Man, this year is going to be awesome!

I also got the list of elective classes I can choose from this year. Elective classes are the fun classes that kind of make up for all of the boring classes we have all year.

So this year I got a choice of:

- [x] **Enchantments and Potions**
- [x] **Zombie Pig Farming**
- [x] **Crafting and Transformations**
- [x] **Minecraft Modding Class**
- [x] **Basket Weaving**
- [x] **7th Grade Student Orientation Volunteering**

There are a lot of great electives to choose from this year. But I think I'm going for the Minecraft Modding Class.

Minecraft Modding Class is where you can learn how to **CREATE MODS** for Minecraft. It's really cool. You can pretty much change anything in Minecraft with a mod.

One time, one of the eighth graders created a mod that changed everybody's voice. All of the Zombies sounded like Endermen, and the Slimes sounded like Skeletons. Even the cows and pigs got reversed.

Another time, one of the mod kids wrote a mod that turned all of the animals **UPSIDE DOWN**! It was really cool. I actually got to ride a Zombie pig upside down that day. Though his little Zombie piggy nipples tickled my legs so much I couldn't stop laughing.

Look at that upside down Pig!

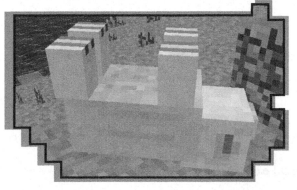

Maybe in Modding Class, I'll create a mod that will help me get revenge on all of the bullies in school. I'll probably make the bullies really small and give the little mob kids really big feet to **SQUASH THEM.** Then we'll see how they like it for a change.

Wow, Minecraft Modding Class is going to be awesome!

My Mom said that if I want to get into a good Mob High School that I should volunteer a lot. They probably think that if you volunteer a lot, then you won't cause any trouble in High School.

So I might volunteer for the 7th Grade Student Orientation. That's when you take a 7th grader and show him around the school, and show him the ropes and stuff.

I guess it would be nice to save some young 7th grade Zombie from having to deal with all the nonsense I went through when I was in 7th grade.

Or maybe I can save a kid from getting too many **ZOMBIE WEDGIES.**

Oh man, Zombie wedgies are not fun. And they usually leave a kid with some serious body image issues.

One time a Zombie kid at school got a wedgie so hard, his feet ended up on his chin. He had to walk around school like that for a whole day. He kinda looked like a Zombie frog.

Another kid got a wedgie so hard that it split him right in half. Wasn't so bad until he tried to catch the bus home. They couldn't find his other half for weeks.

I got a wedgie once. My friend Mutant wanted to play a joke on me. I don't think he really knows how strong he  is. And it didn't help that I wasn't wearing any underwear that day.

I'm still recovering from that.

So, maybe I can help a young 7th grader escape all of the terrors of middle school. Or at least I can be a good friend to him the way Steve was for me.

So, I'm all set with all my classes.

The only thing that scares me is if I'm going to get good teachers this year.

My teachers last year were pretty good. Even Ms. Bones was OK. She was a **LITTLE STIFF,** though.

I guess we'll see.

Eighth grade here I come!

WEDNESDAY

Today we went shopping for school supplies.

This time I didn't even try to ask my Dad to use his Zombie Credit Card. I didn't want the Zombie lady at the counter to think I was a **CRIMINAL** again.

This year we went to Scarget to get our school supplies. If you want to get the best haul for school stuff, that's where you need to go.

Now, the biggest thing I needed this year was a cool Zombie backpack. I'm kind of tired of using the one my Mom made for me.

You see, my Mom has been making my Zombie backpack every year since I was a baby Zombie. I think she does it because it's cheaper to make it out of **ROTTEN ZOMBIE** flesh. It only takes a few months to collect enough around the house to make a good sized backpack.

It's kind of embarrassing, though. All the kids look at me like I'm a weirdo or something. It's probably because my Mom doesn't care what body parts the rotten flesh came from.

One year I had a Zombie backpack that was shaped like my Dad's foot. Another year it was shaped my Mom's entire left leg.

But, now that I'm in eighth grade, I kind of want something a little cooler than a hand me down, rotten flesh, foot-shaped backpack.

What I really want is an authentic, genuine **ENDER DRAGON-HIDE** leather backpack. Those are really cool. But they're really rare. And they're crazy expensive. Usually only the really rich Endermen kids at school carry those.

An Ender Dragon-hide backpack has like 100 pockets. You can stash a year's supply of dried booger snacks in there and never run out. Plus, the teachers can't search every pocket, so you can get away with carrying all kinds of stuff in there.

One year, one mob kid was selling extra Zombie fingers at school, and he kept his stash in his Ender Dragon-hide back pack. The teachers could never catch him.

So cool.

I know I can never get one. But a kid can dream...

I also needed to get some supplies for my Mob Scare Class.

This year I really wanted to get some cool stuff for **SCARING MINERS.**

Last year, some eighth grade kids got megaphones to make their voices louder in the caves. Another time, I saw one kid with one of those cool electronic Voice Changing megaphones. You know, the ones that make you sound like you're a Zombie robot. You can also use it to make yourself sound like an Enderman, a Ghast, or even a chicken.

You know, if I had one of those, I would make myself sound more human. I could trick the miners into coming real close, and then I would jump out from behind a rock and scare them.

Man, I could get SO MANY emeralds that way.

But, my Mom and Dad don't like spending a lot of money on school supplies. So, they just got me my usual wooden pickaxe and shovel. Somehow my Mom and Dad still think that humans are scared by a bunch of **GROWLING, BANGING, AND SCRATCHING** noises.

Sometimes I feel like my parents just don't understand.

And miners aren't easy to scare either. They're real tough.

Last year, I heard that an eighth grader tried to scare a miner one night with his little pickaxe, shovel, and growling combo. The miner used the pickaxe to pick his teeth and used the shovel to knock off the Zombie's head.

...And they still haven't found it.

It's a good thing his Mom had a spare. It's not the same size though. So when he walks around school, he looks really weird.

The only thing I couldn't get today was a lunchbox. They ran out of the lunchbox I wanted. I wanted the cool Pokémon Lunchbox with Pikachu on the front.

But Mom said she would pick it up another day.

So I'm **ALL SET** for school.

But, even though I have most of my stuff, I still feel like I'm going into eighth grade so unprepared.

Maybe I can borrow some of Steve's eighth grade school supplies. Since he's going to ninth grade at his new High School, I don't think he'll need his old eighth grade stuff.

Man, it must be really **WEIRD** going to a new school, and going into the ninth grade. Steve must be really nervous.

You know, maybe I should go check on him to see how he's doing.

☀ THURSDAY ☀

Today my parents gave me a lecture about what it means to be an eighth grade Zombie in middle school.

I kind of felt weird getting advice from my parents about middle school. They're just...you know...old.

But they control all of my money so I kind of had to listen.

First they talked to me about something called, **"SENIOR-ITIS."**

"Senior-what? What's that?"

"Son, that's when you will want to get lazy because you know it's your last year of middle school," my Dad said.

"That's a thing? Really?"

"Yes, it is," Mom said. "And your father and I wanted to help you to do your best in school this year. So we decided that if you get at least a B in each of your classes, then we'll get you any **VIDEO GAME CONSOLE** that you want this year."

"What?!! Are you serious?!!"

"And, one of those classes has to be your new Scare Class," my Dad said. "We know you're feeling nervous about scaring miners. But we believe you can do it, son."

Whoa. That means if I get a B in all my classes, I can get the ScareStation 465 or the Z-Box 360, or the Zii—U!

And it's about time too. I'm so tired of using my Dad's old Zintendo 64. The graphics are terrible.

"That sounds great to me," I said.

"Oh, and Zombie, by the way, your school just got a new **SCHOOL BUS,**" Mom said. "So instead of hobbling to school every day, you can take the bus from now on if you like."

School Bus? I heard that the school bus can be pretty dangerous for a middle school Zombie. Steve told me about the school buses at his school. He said that every day, at least one

New way to school

kid has to endure death by a thousand insults.

"Uh... Sure Mom, I'll think about it."

I'm not so sure how excited I am about riding the school bus. But Wow! I can't believe that I can get my own, brand new video game console!

I just have to figure out how to get all B's this semester. Now, I think

I can do it. But, the only class that really worries me is my Scare Class. I heard scaring miners was real tough. And I'm not the scariest Zombie in the world, you know.

I think it's my dimples. They make me look like a **BABY-FACED** Zombie. I just wish that instead of dimples I could have holes in my face like everybody else.

I don't even know who my new Scare Class teacher is. What if he's really tough? Or maybe it's a lady, and she'll be really strict like Ms. Bones.

I hope I get a really cool teacher like Ms. Slimeballs. She's really flexible. Ms. Ghast is alright too. Except she's

always yelling. I heard Mr. Blaze is
pretty cool, but he
can be a **REAL
HOT HEAD**
sometimes.

Oh man, I can
already feel my new
ScareStation 465
slipping through my
fingers.

I've got to get a B in Scare Class no
matter what it takes.

FRIDAY

I went to go see Steve today. I wanted to see how he was feeling about going to 9th grade in a new High School.

I found him crafting some new back to school supplies on his **CRAFTING TABLE.**

"Hey Steve."

"Hey Zombie. What's crackin'?"

"Uh, my knees, I guess."

"No, I mean, how's it going?"

"Oh, it's going good. I just came to see how you're doing. You getting ready for school?"

"Yeah, I'm just crafting some new tools and weapons that I can use for my new classes. I got my **NEW SCHEDULE** and I have to prep for my Zombie Slaughter and Complete Annihilation Class."

"Wha..?"

"Just kidding. What's up?"

"Hey Steve, can I ask you a question?"

"Sure."

"Aren't you really nervous about going into **9TH GRADE?** I mean, you're going to be freshman at a brand new

High School. And, you're going to be one of the youngest kids there."

"Well, I was real nervous at first. I was kind of worried that the kids at the new school wouldn't like me because of my **SQUARE HEAD.** Most of the kids in that school are Villager kids. And I was kind of feeling self-conscious because I have a really small nose."

"You have a nose? Ah man. That was the only part about your face I liked."

"Ha, ha, you're funny, Zombie. But, you know, I'm not nervous about going to the 9th grade anymore."

"Really? I'm only going to the eighth grade and I'm **REALLY NERVOUS.**"

"Well, I was talking to Alex and she set me straight. I feel much better about it now."

"Really? Because whenever I sit straight, I just feel weird. Makes me feel like I'm human or something."

"No, not *sit straight*. She *set me straight*. It means that she talked to me and it helped me think about things differently."

"Wow. What did she say?"

"She just asked me, 'What are some **REALLY COOL** things you'll miss out on if you never go to the 9th grade?'"

"That's it?"

"Then I thought about all the cool new friendships I would miss out on if I didn't go the 9th grade. I also thought about all the cool new stuff I would miss learning. And then I thought about how much fun it would be to get into **TROUBLE IN HIGH SCHOOL**—but I would totally miss out on it if I never went to the 9th grade."

"Whoa. Alex is like, so deep."

"Chyah, I know."

Wow, after talking to Steve, it made me think of all of the cool things that I would miss out on if I didn't go to the eighth grade.

I would miss out on finally being in the oldest grade at my school and getting respect.

I would miss out on all of the new eighth grade friends I would make.

I would totally miss seeing all of my mob friends go through puberty. Some really crazy stuff happens to mobs when they go **THROUGH PUBERTY.** And I wouldn't want to miss that for the world.

I would miss being with my ghoulfriend Sally through eighth grade, too.

But most of all, I would miss my parents getting me a new ScareStation 465 for passing all of my classes.

Wow. Maybe going to eighth grade isn't **AS BAD** as I thought it would be.

SATURDAY

I had a weird dream today.

It was the last day of school, and I was about to take my final **SCARE EXAM.** This was the test that would determine if I would pass my Scare Class.

I don't know why, but for some reason I was in my underwear. But I didn't care because I was more worried about missing my exam.

When I got to the hallway going toward my class, I started hobbling really fast. But the faster I hobbled, the longer the hallway got.

It took forever to get to my class, but I finally made it to the door...

When all of a sudden, the bell rang. And all of the mob kids started flooding out of my Scare Class.

Oh no. I missed the test!

I walked into the classroom and my teacher looked at me with a look of total disappointment. Then he handed me my report card and it had a **BIG, FAT F** on it!

Suddenly, a big hole opened up on floor and sucked me into a giant vortex. Then a giant ScareStation 465 console appeared and started talking to me.

"Zombie, why didn't you study harder? Why didn't you prepare? You could've done better, Zombie—now we will never be together."

Then it reached out its **VIDEO GAME CONTROLLER** hand to me. Right when I was about to grab it, it got sucked into the vortex.

"NNNNOOOOOOOO!!!!!!!" I yelled.

Then I woke up.

I looked at the clock and realized I had overslept for my first day of school!

I got all my new clothes on. I got my wooden pickaxe and shovel and I shoved them into my Zombie rotten flesh backpack.

I ran downstairs. My Mom and Dad were eating breakfast. I didn't have time for breakfast so I just ran out the door. Then I **HOBBLED** all the way to school.

The only thing I could think about was passing my Scare Class exam no matter what it took. My ScareStation 465 depended on it!

But, when I got to school, it was closed!

My worst nightmare had come true! I had slept straight through the entire semester and missed my entire eighth grade year.

I collapsed on the school stairs and started crying.

"WAAAAAAHHHHH!!!!"

Then Old Man Jenkins came hobbling by.

"What's bugging ya, Zombie?"

"I...can't...get...my...Scare...Station...Four... Sixty...Five...be...cause...I...missed...the... entire...school...year!!! Waaaaaaahhhh!!!!"

I don't know about you, but I have a real hard time talking when I'm crying.

"Whatcha talkin' about, Zombie? School doesn't start till Monday."

Then I realized...it was **SATURDAY.**

So I started giggling hysterically and then I hobbled home.

All I could see when I looked back was Old Man Jenkins shaking his head.

When I got home, I went up to my room and collapsed on my bed.

Man, that was close! I thought. *I'm gonna need to do whatever it takes to pass my Scare Class this year. But what can I do to prepare?*

I started **MAKING SCARY FACES** in the mirror to see if I could make myself look scarier.

Then I thought, *Why don't I just go out and practice scaring some miners tonight?*

All I could think about was my ScareStation 465. So I decided to go for it.

Miners, you better watch out, because here I come!

☀ SUNDAY ☀

Today I spent the whole day in the **MOB HOSPITAL** until my Mom and Dad returned with my head.

I can't really remember what happened.

Only thing I can remember is jumping out at a miner last night. Next thing I know I'm staring at my body lying in the hospital bed without a head.

My head is lonely

It's a good thing they found my head too. If not, I would've had to use the spare. And the only spare my Mom had was a really big one she got at a garage sale the other day. And that thing is the size of a basketball.

Man, I would've had to go to my first day of school tomorrow looking like a **ZOMBIE LOLLIPOP.**

Talk about embarrassing.

When I got home, even though my Mom and Dad were mad, they just told me to get ready for my first day of school tomorrow.

So, the first thing I did was take all of the broken pieces of my pickaxe and shovel and throw them in my Zombie backpack.

The next thing I did was to take out my new turquoise T-shirt and blue pants.

Aw man! My clothes were just too clean to go to school like that. I was going to have to get them **REALLY DIRTY** if I wanted to look my best tomorrow.

So I took my new clothes, and my old clothes, and I threw them in the dirt dryer. I had never used the dirt dryer before. But I saw Mom use it a ton of times.

Hey, I'm a big Zombie now. I'm sure I can handle it.

So I threw all my clothes in and stared at the dirt dryer console. It had some buttons and a big dial. I just pressed the red buttons because that's my favorite color. The dial said something like

- ☒ **Gentle**
- ☒ **Medium**
- ☒ **Max**
- ☒ **Super Max**

The **SUPER MAX** had a skull and cross bones under it so I used that one. It reminded me of Skelee.

I'm going to look so good tomorrow, I thought. I'll probably be the best looking eighth grader in school.

Before I went to bed, I made sure to set my alarm clock so I can get up really early. I wanted to get up right when the sun went down. That way I'd have plenty of time to get everything ready for school.

Man, I felt so excited and so nervous at the same time.

Kind of reminded me of when I gave my ghoulfriend Sally flowers for the first time. Except this time there was no giant **IRON GOLEM** trying to kill me.

At least I don't think so... I haven't even met my new Scare Class teacher yet.

EARLY M✴NDAY

Today was the worst first day of school I have ever had in my entire life.

I think somebody somewhere put a curse on me.

Nothing could've gone any more wrong.

I think I'm going to go run away and become a **ZOMBIE HERMIT** somewhere.

It all started when I woke up this morning.

When my alarm went off, I went to the window to get some fresh night air. But as soon as I opened the curtains, a blast of sunlight hit me right in the face.

Next thing you know my head caught on fire.

After my Mom put it out, I realized I set my alarm clock way too early.

The good thing is that it wasn't as bad as it sounds. I only burned off half of my face.

My Mom gave me a little of her **GREEN ZOMBIE MAKEUP** to cover it up.

Except now I have even more of a Zombie baby face. My face is as smooth as a human baby's bottom.

Then I went to get my clothes from the dirt dryer. Except, when I opened up the dryer, my clothes were gone. I asked my Mom if she took them, but she hadn't seen them either.

I stuck my hand in the dryer to see if they got stuck somewhere.

Then I pulled out a tiny shirt and a tiny pair of pants that looked like they belonged to an action figure.

"MOM!!!!!"

"Honey, what's the matter?"

"My clothes... Look!!!"

"Oh dear."

"WAAAAHHHHH!!!!"

"Maybe we can stretch them out a bit...they might still fit," Mom said hesitantly. "Or you can just wear your old clothes to school."

Then I stuck my hand in the dryer and pulled out my shrunken old clothes.

"Oh dear."

"Waaaaahhhhh!!!!"

At that point, I thought it couldn't get any worse. Boy, was I wrong.

So I squeezed into my mini turquoise T-shirt and mini blue pants. I felt like I was getting a **WEDGIE,** except all over my body.

I got all my stuff together and waddled downstairs, and found my Mom preparing my lunchbox.

"Mom, what's that?!!"

"It's the lunchbox you wanted, right?"

"No, you were supposed to get the **POKÉMON LUNCHBOX** with Pikachu!"

"This one has Pikachu, doesn't it? The lady at the store said it was the most popular one."

"That lunch box is pink! And that's Pichu, not Pikachu! Waaaaahhhhh!!!!"

Now I've got to walk around school with a pink Pichu lunchbox. I might as well accept that my life is over. I should just take a marker and write the word "Loser" on my shirt with a big arrow pointing to my smooth face. Except nobody will be able to read it because my shirt is so small!

"Waaaaahhhhh!!!!"

"Sorry, honey. Why don't you use this lunchbox today and I promise we'll get you a new one next week."

"Waaaaahhhh!!!!"

Now I really thought things couldn't any worse.

I grabbed my lunchbox and my stuff and I hobbled outside. Right before I got out the door my Mom said, "You can catch the school bus down the street. But, make sure you catch the right bus. The color of your bus is gre..."

I was so angry I just **SLAMMED THE DOOR** behind me.

Then I hobbled down the street in my tight outfit. It was really hard to walk. Especially because I couldn't put my arms down. I couldn't bend my knees either so I just bounced on the heels of my feet to walk. I looked like a big "X" just bouncing left and right down the street.

My awkward hobble

I made it to the corner and looked down the street to where I was supposed to go. I saw the **BUS STOP** and it looked like it was a mile away.

As I was getting closer, I saw a grey bus turning the corner!

My bus! I started bouncing faster and faster. All of a sudden I hit a rock and I fell over, and I **LANDED FLAT** on my face.

I tried to get up, but I couldn't. All I could do was make noises until somebody would pick me up.

"MMRRRMMMRRRR!!!!"

Finally somebody saw me and picked me up. It was Old Man Jenkins.

"Zombie, watcha doing playing around on the floor? You're gonna miss your bus."

"Thanks, Mr. Jenkins."

I bounced a few more feet and I saw the bus pulling up. I caught it just in time.

As I looked back I could see Old Man Jenkins shaking his head again.

So as I sat on the bus, I found it kind of weird that we were going in a different direction than my school. But I just thought maybe we had to pick up more kids from other neighborhoods. I also found it kind of weird that only **LITTLE KIDS** were getting on the bus.

I was lying on all the seats in the back of the bus because I couldn't bend my legs to sit down. And since I missed an hour of sleep, I was tired. So I thought I would take a **SHORT NAP.**

"Wake up, buddy!" the bus driver said. "Last stop."

"Whhuzzatt?"

"Last Stop," he said again.

"A little help, please?"

The bus driver helped me get off the bus and then he drove away, laughing, I think.

When I looked up, I knew I was in trouble. The sign read:

PANSY MOB
PRIMARY SCHOOL

Oh man, I had gotten on the wrong bus!

"Waaaahhhhh!!!!"

I just fell on the ground and
STARTED CRYING. I tried
curling up into a ball, but I couldn't
move my arms and legs, so I just lay
there.

Then Old Man Jenkins came galloping
up on his Zombie horse.

"Zombie, you got on the wrong bus.
Your school bus is the green one."

"Waaaahhhhh!!!!!"

"Lucky for you I chased your bus here.
C'mon, I'll give you **A RIDE TO
SCHOOL.**"

"A little help, please..."

Old Man Jenkins picked me up and put me on his Zombie horse. But every time he went to get on I would fall off the other side.

After about **30 MINUTES** of trying to get me on the Zombie horse, he just laid me flat on his Zombie horse and sat on top of me.

So here I am. I'm outside of the Principal's office, writing in my journal, and waiting to hear what's going to happen to me.

It's after lunch time, because I came so late and I missed my first few classes.

But I'm glad I missed lunch. I didn't want anyone laughing at my pink lunchbox anyway.

I hope the Principal just **SENDS ME HOME.** After everything that happened to me today, things just couldn't get any worse...

MONDAY NIGHT

Boy was I wrong...

The Principal decided not to send me home, so I had to finish the rest of my classes today.

My next class was the class I was dreading the most...SCARE CLASS 201.

I bounced into class as all the kids started giggling around me. Big Mouth Jeff was there and he started laughing at me, and his friends joined in too.

The teacher hadn't arrived yet, so I took the time to try and bend my legs so I could get into one of the desk chairs.

I think I heard something **CRACK.** Then I heard another crack. Suddenly I could bend my legs and fit in my chair.

After all of the kids were in their seats, the strangest looking Zombie walked in the door.

I could swear I heard a 'Gong' as he entered the room.

"My name is Mr. Matsumoto, and I will be your Scare instructor this semester."

Mr. Matsumoto was kind of short, but you could tell every inch of him was just solid muscle...rotten Zombie muscle I mean. He looked at the kids like he could see through their heads. Even the kids that had holes in their heads were scared.

I asked one of the kids next to me about him. "Hey, who is this guy? Where's he from, anyway?"

"That's **MASTER KEN MATSUMOTO.** He's the all-time Moblympics Scare champion for 10 years in a row. He's retired now and teaches middle school as a hobby."

"I DID NOT SAY YOU COULD TALK!"
Mr. Matsumoto boomed. "What is your name?" he asked me.

Gulp. "My name is Zack, but my friends call me Zombie."

"Well, Zombie-san, there is no talking in my classroom. Do you understand?"

"Yes...gulp...sir."

Then Mr. Matsumoto began laying down the ground rules.

"We will start this semester with a Scare exam that will determine if you should even be in this class. If you **FAIL THIS TEST,** the most you will get in this class is a D, because you will not be able to keep up. Do I make myself clear?"

"Yes, Mr. Matsumoto."

"The exam will test your ability to scare miners, the most difficult and ruthless villagers around."

What? I couldn't believe my ears.

"The exam will be next week. It will be one part written and one part scaring. You must pass both parts to pass this exam. Am I understood?"

"Yes, Mr. Matsumoto."

"Those of you who know you do not have what it takes to scare miners, should save yourselves the trouble, and just pick up a **CLASS DROP** form from my desk at the end of the class. You can ask the Principal to put you an easier class, like Zombie Pig farming. Am I understood?"

"Yes, Mr. Matsumoto."

When class was over I saw half the class get one of the forms from Mr. Matsumoto's desk. I was going to grab one too, but then I could hear my Mom and Dad in my head...

"If you get at least a "B" in every class, ESPECIALLY YOUR SCARE CLASS, we will buy you the ScareStation 465."

So I decided not to grab a form, and try to pass the class on my own.

But as I was walking out of the classroom, Mr. Matsumoto stopped me, took a form from his desk and **SHOVED IT** into my back pack.

Man, talk about a vote of confidence...

TUESDAY

Well, while I was at school yesterday my Mom picked up some **NEW CLOTHES** for me.

It was a good thing she did too. She had to cut me out of my Mini-me outfit. And when she cut open my pant legs, both of my legs fell on the floor.

So that's what those cracks were that I heard yesterday...

Also, my body was in a really weird shape.

"Aw Mom. Everybody is going to think I got a wedgie."

"Don't worry, Zombie, it'll wear off...in about a week."

"Uuuurrgghhh!!!!"

Mom said she couldn't get me a **NEW LUNCHBOX** because they were all sold out. I had to wait a few more weeks for a new one.

Great, now everybody is going to see my pink lunchbox.

We have to carry a lot of books to school, so I couldn't fit my lunchbox in my Zombie backpack. Now I have to go to school today with a new turquoise T-shirt and blue pants—and a pretty pink lunchbox hanging off my backpack.

Life is so unfair.

One good thing that happened today is that I had my **MINECRAFT MODDING** Class.

When we got into class, the teacher was talking about how you can use a mod to change anything in Minecraft. The only thing is that the mod's effect is only temporary. So it only lasts a few hours.

We were only allowed to do basic mods. The really advanced ones were too dangerous for kids, and only the military and the programmers at Mojang were allowed to use those.

So with our mods, we could only change the color of our clothes, or change the shape of small objects.

But we weren't allowed to turn animals upside down. That was done by **A HACKER** named "Grumm," who was a student at our school a few years back. He got kicked out of school for using that mod though.

"I wonder if we can use a mod to cheat on Mr. Matsumoto's Scare exam," said a **WITHER SKELETON** kid named Jesse.

"Yeah, we could probably make ourselves look even scarier and make our voices really loud," said a Slime boy named Billy.

"Yeah, but we need a special mod to do that. They won't allow us to that kind of mod at school," said a Creeper kid named Leo.

Wow, that's a really good idea, I thought. *With my baby face, I don't think I can scare anybody. But if I had a mod like that, it would really help me scare some miners.*

What am I thinking? That would be cheating. It wouldn't be right.

But it sure would make getting my ScareStation 465 a whole lot easier...

At lunchtime it was great seeing all of my old friends again.

Skelee was there, and so was Creepy and Slimey.

"Hey guys!"

"WASSUP ZOMBIE!"

"Wow, I really missed you guys. Did you guys have fun this summer?"

"Sure did!" Slimey said. "I got a chance to see my family in the Super Flat Biome. I also got a chance to practice my bouncing. I'm really good at it now, like really good."

"I got a chance to see where my family was from," Skelee said. "Did you know that Yellowbone National Park was originally named after my great, great, grandfather? Mt. Skullmore even has his picture carved into the stone."

"Really, your grandfather was a president?"

"Well, he's not at the top. He's somewhere toward the middle I think."

"Zombie and I had a lot of fun at **CREEPAWAY CAMP,**" Creepy said. "We even won the Camp Moblympics!"

"For real?"

"Yeah, but that was because Creepy really came through and won it for us," I said.

Man, it was really good seeing the guys again.

And the thing I said about puberty was true. They all look **SO DIFFERENT** now.

Skelee has longer arms and legs. It looks kind of funny because his spine hasn't grown very much. I think he even started dragging his knuckles on the ground like a gorilla.

Slimey got really big too. He was big before, but he never had a problem getting through doors. Now, he has to enter the school through the back loading dock.

But the one that's really changed is Creepy. His neck is longer than ever.

All of us are looking up at him now. It's really weird.

Creepy told us **HIS FARTS** have gotten worse since he's gone through puberty. I think it's because of the gun powder in his system.

But since none of us have noses, we really don't mind.

WEDNESDAY

I had Spelling class today and the weirdest thing happened.

The teacher asked someone in the class to spell "**OBSIDIAN**" and no one knew how to spell it.

So I raised my hand and spelled it out for her.

Then she asked someone to spell the word 'Enchantment.' None of the kids volunteered so I raised my hand and spelled that one out too.

Then she asked the class to spell the word 'Shepherd' and I raised my hand.

"S-H-E-Uh...Um... P-E-R-D?"

"Sorry, Zombie, that's incorrect. Can anyone else spell 'Shepherd'?"

Then Big Mouth Jeff raised his hand and spelled it right.

It's just like Jeff, always trying to be better than me.

Well, the teacher asked both of us to stay after class. She said that they were going to have a **SPELLING BEE** coming up in a few weeks, and she asked us if we wanted to join it. She said the competition will decide who will represent the school in the national Minecraft Spelling Bee with all the different Biomes.

Now, I didn't really want to do it, but when I saw how quickly Big Mouth Jeff jumped in and said yes, I had to jump in too.

There's no way I'm going to let Jeff beat me at anything!

The good thing is that we get **EXTRA CREDIT** for being part of the Spelling Bee. So it will help me get an easy "A" in Spelling class.

Later, we had our Scare class again, and man was it intense.

Mr. Matsumoto took all of us into the mines so that we could get first-hand experience of how to scare miners.

He said that everything we learned today would be on our Scare exam coming up in a few days.

I'll be honest, I'm really scared of the miners. Last time I met a miner, I got my head knocked clean off.

The other kids were really scared too. The only one that wasn't scared was Mr. Matsumoto.

Then we heard a noise that sounded like people **SINGING** and **SWINGING** pickaxes. We all jumped back behind some rocks and stayed hidden.

"Children, today I am going to demonstrate the proper form of how to scare a miner," Mr. Matsumoto said. "So watch closely."

Mr. Matsumoto sneaked up **REAL CLOSE** to the miners. All of us were shaking in our boots. Then Mr. Matsumoto did something weird. It looked like he was taking a deep breath (which is funny because Zombies don't have any lungs.) Then all of a sudden he jumped out from behind the rocks at the miners.

"HYEEEEAAAAAHHHHUURRRGHH-HHZZZOOWWIIIEEEE!!!!"

He was yelling and acting like a crazy person.

But man, those miners turned completely white. One of them just fainted on the spot. Another one turned around so fast to run, he didn't see the wall in front of him. He ran right into it. The last one started screaming like a little girl and waving his hands in the air. He **DROPPED THE EMERALDS** he was holding and took off.

Mr. Matsumoto picked up the emeralds, some Lapis Lazuli, Redstone, some pickaxes, and he even found a diamond sword.

"That's how it is done, children."

Mr. Matsumoto was so awesome that we were all clapping and yelling and screaming and stuff. They said he was a **LEGEND,** and now I know why.

"So you will all be tested on your form, intensity, discipline and control. Remember what you saw here. Class dismissed."

All the kids were **SUPER CRAZY** with excitement over what they just saw.

I have to be honest, so was I.

I know I need to try that out, like today.

I wonder if Steve is going to be out mining tonight...

Later, I went over to see if I could try Mr. Matsumoto's move on Steve.

Luckily, Steve mines **AT NIGHT** a lot. I think he likes the peace and quiet. Or he just likes finding the leftover cake the early miners leave behind.

Then I saw Steve. I think he found some **IRON ORE** because he was banging on that rock pretty hard. It was great for me because he couldn't hear me coming.

When I got up really close, I jumped out from behind the rocks.

"HYEEEEAAAAAHHHHUURRRGHH-HHZZZOOWWIIIEEEE!!!!" I yelled.

But Steve just looked at me and **SMILED.**

"HYEEEEAAAAAHHHHUURRRGHH-HHZZZOOWWIIIEEEE!!!!" I yelled.

Then Steve scratched his head and smiled at me again.

I said it one more time, but Steve just looked at me and smiled a third time.

Then I asked him why he wasn't scared.

Next thing I know he pulled out his earphones and said, "What'd you say?"

Figures. I had to scare the only miner that mines to **MUSIC.**

"I just said that I have a Scare exam that I think I'm going to totally fail."

All of a sudden all my expectations of having my very own, brand new ScareStation 465 started to slowly **FADE AWAY...**

THURSDAY

Today was the first day of my 7th Grade Orientation Volunteer assignment.

But man, I was really **NERVOUS.**

You see, I had the weirdest dream last night.

I was showing one of the new 7th Grade mob kids around. He was a really nice kid, except he was a Creeper and he was really nervous.

Everywhere I took him, he started hissing and flashing. It's like he was afraid of everything.

I took him to the library... HSSSSSS.

I took him to the gym.... HSSSSSS.

I took him to the cafeteria... HSSSSS.

I showed him the study hall...
HSSSSSS

I finally stopped and asked him why he was **SO NERVOUS.** He said he was afraid that the other kids wouldn't like him. Then he said he was afraid he couldn't handle the workload. Then he said he was afraid he was going to get bullied.

I thought I would help him overcome his fear. So I took him on the school bus.

Next thing I know, after the explosion, I had Creeper juice all over me.

Last thing I remember was **YELLING** at the top of my voice... and then I woke up.

Wow, I forgot how hard it was to be a 7th grader.

Thinking back on it, I probably wouldn't have made it as a 7th grader if it wasn't for having a friend like Steve around.

So I guess it's my turn to be a 'Steve' for some other goofy kid.

Now the kid I had to show around was a really cool Zombie kid named Neville.

Neville was a transfer student from the **AUSTRALIAN BIOMES.**

Even though he was a little different, Neville was pretty cool. Plus he was really outgoing.

In fact, he had already started making friends by the time I met him. All the teachers and secretaries in the school office already knew him. And when we walked down the hallway, all the kids said "what's up?" to him. He would just say, **"G'DAY"** to the girls and they would run giggling down the hall.

To be honest, I started getting a little jealous. This kid had only been in school two days and he already had a ton of friends.

"How come you know so many people already?" I asked him.

"Ah mate, we **AUSSIES** know that if you don't have your mates, you've only got a party with one person. And there's no fun in that."

I really had no idea what he just said, but it sounded so cool.

Man, no wonder he's got so many friends. It's probably his accent.

Later that day, I saw some of the cool kids hanging around the water fountain and I thought I would try my new accent.

"G'day there mates.

OWYAGOING?"

Well, it didn't work out as well as I expected.

...Took me a little while to find my way out of that dumpster.

FRIDAY

I'm really excited because my ghoulfriend Sally comes back tomorrow.

She was excused from the first week of school because her parents **DONATE** money to the school.

They even have a building at school named after Sally's dad. It's called the Abner Cadaver Performing Arts Building. I think he was a magician when he was younger or something.

So because Sally's dad donates so much money to the school, Sally can get away with a lot of stuff other kids can't.

She actually missed about **28 DAYS** of school last year and didn't get in trouble. But it wasn't like she was cutting class—it was more like she was cutting her fingernails.

I wanted to spend more time with her this weekend, but I needed to study for this crazy Scare exam that's happening next week.

I've got to do whatever it takes to pass this test, though I'm not feeling really confident about it.

The kids at school were talking about using a mod to cheat on the Scare exam again. They even found out where the hacker Grumm, who got expelled, lives.

They said they just needed to come up with the money to pay him and he'll program the mod for them. They said that the mod would make them even scarier than Mr. Matsumoto.

Those guys keep asking me if I want to join them... But I don't know. I've never cheated before. And if my parents ever found out, they would be so disappointed in me. Not to mention I would be grounded **FOR THE REST OF MY LIFE.**

I just need to find a way to pass this Scare exam. I just need to.

My gaming career depends on it.

SATURDAY

I went to see Steve to ask if maybe he could help me pass the Scare Exam.

"Scaring villagers is easy," I told him. "But miners are real tough."

"You don't have to tell me. Miners are the roughest, **TOUGHEST** villagers around. Those guys don't take anything from anybody. Not even Zombies."

"So what am I going to do? If I don't pass this test, the most I can get is a D in the class. And if I do that, my Mom and Dad will never get me the ScareStation 465."

"Yeah, that's a tough one, Zombie. What are you going to do?"

"Well, some of the kids at school were thinking of **USING A MOD** to make themselves scarier, and they asked me to join them."

"Wait a minute... Isn't that cheating?"

"Well... Yeah, but **TECHNICALLY** it'll still be us, just a different version."

"Zombie. I'm your friend. So I'm not going to tell you what to do. But... Don't do it!"

"But how am I supposed to pass this scare exam? You said it yourself.

Miners are tough. And look at my face. Those miners will take one look at me and laugh, and then they'll **KNOCK MY HEAD OFF.**"

"Yeah, well maybe a ScareStation 465 is not worth the price you're going to pay if you do cheat on your exam. Not to mention that if you get caught, you'll get expelled. Then what are your gonna do?"

"I can't think about that right now. I just need to pass this test."

"Zombie, **DON'T DO IT,** man. You're better than that," Steve said.

"Well, I gotta go see Sally. So I'll see you later."

Man, I knew Steve was right. But I just have to pass this test...I just have to.

Later, I went to see Sally at her house.

She lives in a 27 bedroom house on an island on the other side of the lake. Actually, Sally's family owns the whole island.

When I got there, the **ZOMBIE BUTLER** opened the door. I don't think he likes me much. He keeps calling me Zeke.

"Sally, your little friend Zeke is here."

"Zombie!" Sally said when she saw me. And she gave me a big hug.

"Hey Sally," I said. "I missed you a lot. How was your trip?"

"Oh, it was OK. I've done that trip like **7 YEARS** in a row now so it was the same old thing."

"Cool."

We spent the day talking about school and my first day.

"Zombie, you're so funny. The craziest things always happen to you."

"Yeah, I think somebody put a curse on me or something. I just wish they had cursed my face so that I would be a bit scarier."

"What? I like your baby Zombie, little **BOOBLY, WOOBLY FACE,**" she said as she pinched my cheek.

"Ha ha. That's not funny, Sally. I have a really tough Scare exam coming up, and I don't think I'm going to pass. And if I fail, my parents aren't going to get me my ScareStation 465."

"Oh, I played one of those. I even played the ScareStation 466. It's not coming out till next year."

Great, at this rate, I'm going to miss the ScareStation 465 and the 466. I'll probably only get to play a ScareStaion when I'm Old Man Jenkin's age.

"I don't know, Sally. I need to do whatever it takes to pass that Scare exam."

"You don't mean **CHEATING,** do you?"

"Yeah... Some of the kids want to use mods to make ourselves look **SCARIER** for our Scare exam."

Sally looked at me like I was a lost puppy that needed a home. She always had a way of making me feel like she really understood.

"You know, Zombie, if you cheat and you pass the Scare exam, and you get your ScareStation 465, it's not really going to matter."

"Why?"

"Because you're gonna **FEEL SO BAD** every time you play it, that you'll never be able to enjoy it...Plus the 466 is much better anyway."

Wow. That was really deep.

Man, I'm **REALLY LUCKY** to have a ghoulfriend like Sally. She really knows how to make me feel worse than ever about cheating on this Scare exam.

But right now I don't feel like I have any other choice...

What to do?

* SUNDAY *

So those other guys at school called me today to ask me if I was going to join them and cheat on the Scare exam.

Even though I know Steve and Sally are right, I just know I can't pass this Scare exam on my own.

So I told those guys I would join them.

They said it would cost **10 BUCKS** each so that we could pay Grumm to create the mod for us.

I still had a little of my **ALLOWANCE MONEY** left because I was saving up for a new Zintendo 64 video game. But if this works, I guess I'm not going to need it anyway.

So I told them I was going to bring the money to school tomorrow.

Wow, this was going to be the first time I ever cheated on a school exam.

I've thought about cheating before, and a lot of the other kids at school cheated. But I never have.

Man, I'm feeling really weird right now.

It's kind of like a mixture of **FEAR AND EXCITEMENT** and diarrhea all at the same time.

...I think I'm just going to go take a nap.

M✱NDAY

Today in Scare Class Mr. Matsumoto was doing a review for the Scare exam.

"You all have to be able to scare one miner each. And only the following **THREE THINGS** count as a scare:

1. The miner turns a different color. White, blue, green or purple are the preferred colors, but red will qualify as well.

2. The miner faints. If he is faking, it doesn't count. And if you scare him while he is

sleeping, that doesn't count either.

3. The miner runs away. And extra points will be awarded if he runs into a wall or trips over a rock on the way out.

Do I make myself clear?"

"Yes, Mr. Matsumoto."

One kid had a **DEATH WISH** and he asked Mr. Matsumoto a dumb question: "Mr. Matsumoto, what if instead of running away the miner **TURNS AROUND** and attacks us?"

Mr. Matsumoto just picked up a dropout form and handed it to the mob boy that asked the question.

"Any more questions?"

All of us were too terrified to ask him anything.

After class, I went with the other mob kids that were going to cheat to the empty Modding Class room.

Jesse, the **MASTERMIND** behind our cheating caper, pulled out a piece of paper from his pocket.

"Here it is, boys. The mod program we need to pass the Scare test. You guys got the cash?"

So we all gave him 10 bucks.

Then he got on the teacher's computer and started typing away and building the mod program we needed.

I was really scared a teacher would walk in on us. And I could tell the two other mob kids were really scared too.

"Alright guys. Now each of you has to **TYPE YOUR NAME** into the mod."

The first boy typed in his name. Then the second boy typed in his name.

When it was my turn, I knew that once I typed in my name there was no turning back. I must've waited for what seemed like an hour.

"Hurry up, Zombie, the Modding Class teacher can walk in any minute."

Z-A-C-K _ Z-O-M-B-I-E

Wow. I can't believe I did it. I feel so...soiled.

"Well, it's finished," Jesse said. "I uploaded it to my cell phone. So, when it's our turn to take the Scare exam, I just have to **ACTIVATE IT** on my phone, and we're home free."

Wow. That was it? I thought it would be a lot more exciting than that.

"I'll see you guys in the mines," Jesse said as he walked out of the classroom.

After we all walked out, I heard the other two guys talking.

"I'm really scared, Billy. If I get caught, my Dad is going to really let me have it."

"Don't worry, Leo. Jesse's got this. Plus if we get caught, we can always get another mod that will erase it from our **PERMANENT RECORD.**"

What? If I get caught this goes on my permanent record?

Up to that point, I didn't really know what I should've been feeling. All I know is that whatever I was feeling, it felt terrible.

So I just went home and went to bed.

 TUESDAY

Today my parents went to the First Week of School Parent-Teacher Conference.

I really hate those things. My parents always find a way to make me do more homework after they come home from the PTC.

When they got home, I knew I was going to get **ANOTHER LECTURE** about the perils of something...

"Hey Zombie. Did you eat dinner? How's Wesley?"

"Yeah I did, Mom. Wesley's OK too."

"Zombie, you wouldn't believe it, but we ran into your new Scare teacher, Mr. Matsumoto today."

"Yeah, son, did you know he was the Scare Champion for the past 10 years at the Moblympics?"

"Yeah, I know that, Dad."

"Well, it was a good meeting tonight. Son, we want to talk to you about the **PERILS OF...**"

Here we go again.

"...We want to talk to you about the perils of **CHEATING.**"

Gulp.

"Yes, it seems that there are a lot of kids cheating on their exams nowadays. I guess they feel like the pressures of school are too great, so they use cheating as a way to solve their problems."

Gulp.

"So we wanted to let you know, Zombie, that if you ever feel like the PRESSURE at school is too great, you can always come talk to us."

"Uh, Ok, Mom."

"And Zombie, if you ever feel like things are getting too hard in school, we are always here to help."

"Uh, OK, Dad."

You know, I really wanted to tell them. But I couldn't. I just feel like they would be so disappointed in me.

I really wish I could **TALK** to somebody about it, though.

I can't talk to Steve about it because he'll just tell me not to do it. And I can't talk to Sally because I feel like she'll be really disappointed in me too.

So, it's just me and **MY JOURNAL.**

Man, I feel so alone...

WEDNESDAY

Well, today is the day of my Scare exam.

My stomach was feeling really weird, even after I put it in.

I decided to walk to school today instead of taking the bus. I was hoping I could talk myself out of cheating before I got to school.

On my way there I ran into **OLD MAN JENKINS.**

I guess he could tell something was bothering me.

"Hey there, Zombie, what's troublin' ya?"

"Oh, I don't think you'd understand, Mr. Jenkins."

"Why don't cha try me?"

I didn't really think he would understand, but I told him anyway.

"You know, Zombie, I'm not going to tell you what to do, since you're in **EIGHTH GRADE** and all. But can I ask you sumthin'?"

"Uh huh."

"What's the worse that will happen if you flunk your Scare exam?"

"The most I can get is a D in the class, and then I won't get my Scarestation 465."

"And then what's the worse that will happen?

"I'll be stuck playing my Dad's old Zintendo 64."

"And what's the worse that'll happen if you get caught cheating?"

"I'll get **EXPELLED.** My parent's will ground me for life. I'll lose my allowance. I'll disappoint Steve and Sally."

"And then what's the worse that'll happen?"

"I'll feel really dumb. And I'll be a **TOTAL FAILURE** in my life."

All of a sudden cheating on my Scare exam didn't seem like such a good idea anymore.

"So Zombie, watcha going to do?"

"What I should've done a few days ago," I said determined.

I thanked Old Man Jenkins and ran to school to take my Scare exam.

Except this time when I looked back Old Man Jenkins wasn't shaking his head; he gave me a THUMBS UP instead.

As soon as I got to the school, I found Jesse and told him that I didn't want to cheat. I told him that I was just going to try my best.

"Sorry Zombie. I already programmed all of us into the system. Once I press the button, we'll all get modded. And I'm not failing this exam," he said as he slowly put his fist in my face.

Gulp.

After we took the **WRITTEN PART** of the exam, we took the bus to the mines. All the way there I was trying to think about what to do.

I could tell Mr. Matsumoto, I thought. But then I'll not only be a cheater, I'll also be a big rat tattle tale, too. Not to mention that Jesse will knock my head off.

Oh man, what was I going to do?

We got to the mines and Mr. Matsumoto gave us the last **INSTRUCTIONS** before the exam.

"Alright class. Everyone take a digital camera. Use your cameras to take a picture of your miner after you scare them. This way you can prove you did it. Is that clear? Well then, class, get **ON YOUR MARK!** Get Set! Go!"

We all ran into the mines to find the miner we were going to scare. Since it was mining season, finding the miners was going to be really easy.

When we got deep in the mines, I could see Jesse pull out his phone from a distance. When no one was around, he gave me and the other guys a nod and then he pushed the button.

All of a sudden I started feeling weird and bubbly. Then my body started to grow and grow and grow. My arms got really thick and my legs became the size of TREE TRUNKS. My chest started to bulge out like I had swallowed a mattress.

I tried to talk and I sounded like I swallowed a bag of razor blades.

"RRAAAAAARRRRR!!!!" was all I could say.

Oh man. If a miner sees me like this he'll be scared out of his skin.

Then I heard a noise that sounded like singing and somebody **SWINGING A PICKAXE.**

Maybe if I talk to the miner he would understand, I thought. I'm sure he was a kid in middle school once.

So I slowly walked out from around the corner and went up to the miner.

"RESCUZE ME, MR. MINERRR, SIR. RRAAAARRRR! I JUST RANTED TO RASK YOU IF YOU ROULD KRINDLY..."

"HHHEEEEYAAAAAAAAAHHHHHH!!!!!"

Not only did the miner turn white, but he turned blue, green, purple and red.

Not only did he try to run away, but he ran into the wall, and he went through the wall. Then he **FAINTED.**

Wow. This is what it must feel like to scare a real life miner.

But I knew I didn't deserve the credit. So I took out my camera and I did what I knew I had to do.

Then I took the picture and headed back.

Before we got back to Mr. Matsumoto, Jesse pressed the button on his phone and changed us all back.

All the kids started handing in their **CAMERAS.** Then Jesse, Billy and

Leo handed in their cameras. They were all laughing and high fiving each other.

I was the last one to hand in my camera. And Mr. Matsumoto stood there looking at me really impatiently.

I finally handed him my camera but I didn't say anything. I decided to let the picture do all the talking.

Mr. Matsumoto took one look at the picture I took, and then he smiled. He looked at me and gave me a nod.

"Nice going, ZOMBIE-SAN," he said.

I just smiled back, and instead of taking the bus, I decided to walk home.

✳ THURSDAY ✳

So here I am. My first day of detention.

You're probably wondering how I got here.

Well, I decided to tell **THE TRUTH.** But I had to do it without ratting on Jesse, Billy and Leo.

So, I thought, if a picture is worth a thousand words, I decided to let the picture I took in the mines do all the talking.

I even scare myself!

You see, instead of taking a picture of the scared miner, I decided to take a picture of **MYSELF.**

I told Mr. Matsumoto that I created a mod to change my appearance in order to cheat on the test. But I decided not to go through with it because I had a change of heart.

Mr. Matsumoto was so impressed with **MY HONESTY** that he didn't report me to the principal but gave me detention instead. Now I just stay after school practicing my scare technique with Mr. Matsumoto.

I'm gonna need it too, because Mr. Matsumoto also gave me a chance to retake the Scare exam.

So I still have a chance to get my ScareStation 465.

Oh, and Jesse, Leo and Billy eventually **GOT CAUGHT.**

I heard that on the school bus on the way back from the mines, Jesse started calling his friends and bragging about how he aced his Scare exam. But Leo accidentally bumped into him and

Jesse dropped his phone. When Leo went to go pick it up, he accidentally pressed the mod button on Jesse's phone.

They transformed into giant monster Zombies right inside of the school bus.

The bus got so heavy, it blew out all the tires. Then some of the mob kids started freaking out and jumping out of the school bus windows.

Yeah...they got **EXPELLED.**

Wow, talk about a crazy first few weeks of school...

FRIDAY

Today in the cafeteria, Big Mouth Jeff was bragging about how well he did scaring the miners on his Scare exam.

When he saw me, he started talking about how he was going to beat everyone else at the Spelling Bee.

Man, he just gets me so mad when he acts cocky like that!

I couldn't help it. I just **BLURTED OUT** the first thing that came into my head.

"Well, I bet you won't beat me!"

"Oh yeah, you want to put down a wager on that?"

"Any time, any place!"

"I'll bet you my Zbox 360 that I'll win," Jeff said. "But it won't matter because you don't have anything I want."

All of a sudden the entire cafeteria said a big, "**OOOOOOHHH!!!**"

"Well, how about a ScareStation 465!" I yelled out before I got a chance to think about what I was saying.

Then the entire cafeteria said, "Oooooohhh!!!"

"It's a bet. If I win, I get your ScareStation 465. If you win, you get my Zbox 360."

Then the entire cafeteria said, "Ooooooohhh!!!"

After it was all over, Skelee came over to me and asked really serious like, "You don't have a ScareStation 465 do you?"

"Nope."

"So I guess you'd better win the **SPELLING BEE** then?"

"Yep."

"And you probably don't have any idea how you're going to do that, right?"

"Nope."

"I figured. Alright, I'll get all of the guys together tomorrow so we can figure out some **CRAZY IDEA** to get you out of this situation."

"Yep."

SATURDAY

Today all the guys came together to help me beat Big Mouth Jeff at the Spelling Bee.

Skelee, Creepy, and Slimey were all there. Steve was going to meet up with us later.

"Zombie, you do know that Jeff was last year's student **REPRESENTATIVE** for our school at the National Minecraft Spelling Bee, right?" Skelee asked. "And he was only a 7th grader back then."

Gulp.

"Uh, no, I didn't know that. I just knew that he can spell 'Shepherd.'"

"Zombie, you've got nothing to worry about. You **SPELL GREAT,**" Creepy said.

"Did you just say Zombie 'smells' great?" Skelee said.

"No, I said that Zombie 'spells' great!"

"Uh Oh, Creepy's got that lisp again."

"Stop it, you guys, that's not funny. You know I've been working really hard on it."

All of a sudden, Steve walked up.

"Sup guys!"

"Steve!"

"So, Zombie, I heard you're going up against Big Mouth Jeff for the school Spelling Bee championships."

"Yeah... I'm kinda **NERVOUS** about it."

"You bet something you don't have, didn't you?" Steve asked.

"Uh...yeah."

"Well, let's do this. What's the plan?"

"Help Zombie memorize a bunch of words, I guess," Slimey said.

"Uh, I just have a small problem, you guys. Since I've been going through puberty, I've sort of been losing my memory."

"FOR REAL?"

"Yeah, my Dad said it's because I'm losing the last traces of my baby brain. Kind of like when you lose your baby teeth."

"Does that mean you're going to grow another one?" Steve asked.

"Naw, Dad just said that once a Zombie passes puberty, you just have one **BIG HOLLOW SKULL.** It's great for a nice infestation of grubs, or even a bird's nest."

"Whoa."

"Makes a really cool drum sound if you bang it at the right spot, too."

"So wait a minute. In order to win this Spelling Bee, you've to go memorize like a thousand words...and you're losing your memory?" Skelee asked.

"Uh, yeah."

"Oh OK, just checking. So what's the plan?"

None of us could come up with an idea of how I was going to **BEAT JEFF** at the Spelling Bee.

"Hey, wait a minute," Steve said suddenly. "If you're losing your memory, shouldn't Jeff be losing his too, since he's a Zombie?"

"Well, Jeff is kind of special," I said. "He always has been. For some reason he's always been good at whatever he does. He's pretty much won every competition he's ever been in."

All of us got quiet after the last thing I said.

Man, a **SPELLING MOD** would come in really handy right now...

☀ SUNDAY ☀

"Hey Dad, how come Zombies start losing our memory when we go through puberty?"

"Well, Zombie, when we're born we have a little brain about the size of a walnut. It's supposed to help us to learn most of things we're ever going to need in life. Once we go through puberty, our brains shrink to about the size of a pea."

"So Dad, does that mean you're a 'PEA-BRAIN'?"

"Well, yes, I guess it does, son."

"So then how do you remember really important things that you need to know?"

"Well, son, that's what the **ZOMBIE-NET** is for. You just type in something that you need to remember and there it is."

"What if I wanted to win a contest like a school Spelling Bee?"

"Well, I'm sorry, son, but there are some things we Zombies were just never meant to do in life. Why don't you try Zombie Pig Farming? Zombies have been known to be really great at that."

I could already see my ScareStation 465 going down the vortex, along with the little respect that I could've had as an eighth grader.

But I still don't understand how **BIG MOUTH JEFF** is able to do it. He's a Zombie, so how come he can remember things so well?

You know, if I got a mod that could help me remember things better, I could win the Spelling Bee real easy.

What am I thinking? That's cheating again.

Why is cheating so easy but trying to just get through middle school is so hard?

Man, the life of a 12 year old Zombie has just way **TOO MUCH** drama...

I went to go see Steve later, and I told him about my idea of using a mod to remember things better.

I kind of knew that he was going to tell me not to do it, but I just needed somebody to talk me out of it.

"So what do you think?" I asked Steve.

"I think it's a great idea."

"YOU DO?"

"Not really, but since you're losing your memory, you probably won't remember that we had this conversation."

"C'mon Steve, I'm serious. Really, what do you think?"

"Well, you know, I cheated once, and I got away with it too. I passed my test, and nobody ever found out."

"Are you serious?"

"Yeah, and I've never forgotten it," Steve said with a sad look on his face.

I would've never thought in a **MILLION YEARS** *that Steve would cheat at anything.*

"But, you know Zombie, it's a lot harder to cheat than it is to study."

"What do you mean?"

"Well, you only have to study for a few days to pass a test and then you forget about it. But if you cheat, you have to **REMEMBER IT** for the rest of your life."

Wow. That was deep.

So, I decided to skip the memory mod idea. But I still needed to find a way to win the Spelling Bee.

Well, I may still have enough of my brain to remember some words. Like I bet I can spell Shepherd.

S-H-E-P ... Uh.

Man! I'm still **CHOKING** like I did in Spelling class.

I'm going to need to find a way to remember if I get stuck.

But what am I going to do?

MNDAY

I had detention again today with Mr. Matsumoto.

This time there were 2 other kids there because they had to retake the Scaring exam too. There was a skeleton girl named Tibia and a Slime boy named Erol.

When we got to the classroom, we found **A NOTE** from Mr. Matsumoto telling us to meet him at the school Zombie animal farm.

We went around to the Zombie animal farm in the back of the school. When we got there Mr. Matsumoto was knee deep in mud, making faces at some pigs and sheep. All they did was **STARE BACK** at him.

We just looked at each other, like he was crazy.

"Mr. Matsumoto, what are you doing?"

"When I was a boy in my country, we didn't have fancy training equipment or fancy technology to make us scary. So we had to practice with what **NATURE** provided for us."

Either Mr. Matsumoto was crazy or he really did learn how to scare miners by practicing on pigs and sheep.

"What you need to do is picture in your mind the scariest, ugliest, most hideous human you can imagine. Then you become that human. And when the time is right..."

"HYEEEEEAAAAAAHHHHHUURRRGHH-HHHZZZOOWWIIIIEEEEE!!!!!"

Next thing I know the sheep just fell right over. I thought it was dead.

The pig turned from **PINK TO WHITE** and ran away as fast as it could.

Whoa.

"Zombie-san, you try it."

So I found a sheep and I stared at it for a little bit. Then I yelled:

"HYEEEEEAAAAAAHHHHUURRRGHHH-
HHZZZOOWWIIIIEEEEE!!!!!"

But the sheep just stood there looking
at me.

Come on Sheep, be scared!

"Zombie-san, you have to let it come
from **INSIDE**. Reach in and tap all of
your passion, strength and imagination,
and then let it out!"

This time I took a deep breath, and
I stared at the sheep. I thought

about the scariest, ugliest, most **HIDEOUS HUMAN** I could imagine. I couldn't think of any so I just thought about what Big Mouth Jeff would look like if he was human. And then I imagined Big Mouth Jeff taking my ScareStation 465. All of a sudden I yelled at the top of my voice...

"HYEEEAAAAAHHHHUURRRGHHH-HZZZOOWWIIIIEEEEE!!!!!"

But nothing happened.

Then suddenly, the sheep started leaning over little by little, and then "**PLOP,**" it tipped over like it was dead.

"I did it! Mr. Matsumoto, I did it!"

"Well done, Zombie-san," he said.

Wow, who'd ever think that a baby faced Zombie like me could scare a sheep into **FAINTING.**

I guess I really can do anything if put my mind to it.

Even if it is the size of a pea...

TUESDAY

Today we went on a field trip to the Museum of Mob Natural History.

It was really cool. We got to learn about all of our mob ancestors and how they lived.

Skelee saw a picture of his great, great grandpa **YELLOWBONE** at the Museum. His great, great grandpa was the one they named the Yellowbone National Park after. We found out they called him Yellowbone because he was the only survivor when a Creeper exploded in a highlighter factory.

Slimey learned that according to research Slimes may be a more advanced evolutionary form of snot.

Creepy was really interested in finding out where his ancestors came from. There was a rumor going around that Creepers came from a programming **MISTAKE** at Mojang, when they were trying to make a pig.

But the rumors weren't true. But they do think that Creepers, like Zombies, were part of a human **MILITARY EXPERIMENT** that went wrong. This is what they think Creepers looked like before the experiment:

We got to the Zombie exhibit and they were having a special exhibit called, "What Makes Zombies Tick."

The part that I was really interested in was the "Zombie Pea Brain" exhibit. It showed the inside of a Zombie head and what a Zombie pea brain looks like.

IT WAS AWESOME.

The part that was really cool was what it said about the Zombie brain. It said:

The typical Zombie's "pea-sized" brain, though small, is very powerful. It's kind of like the CPU of a computer. It houses enough information to help a Zombie live a normal Zombie life, but with some limitations.

One of those limitations is a Zombie's inability to maintain long-term memory. It is said that a Zombie can only remember the information that it learned in the first few years of life, or what it heard within **THE LAST 3 HOURS.**

But then it said something that I thought was really interesting. It said:

Though a Zombie's pea-brain is unable to store long-term memory, Zombies have a remarkable sense of imagination. Because of this, Zombies have been known to recall previous information with great accuracy in moments of intense imagination.

There are accounts of Zombies remembering events that happened hundreds of years prior, even though their pea-brain does not have the capability to retain this information.

Though research is still being conducted to explain why this happens, this phenomenon is still unexplained...

Wow. That would explain why my parents always said I have a **WILD IMAGINATION.**

The good thing is that it said that I can remember things I hear in the past 3 hours. So I guess I'll just have to study 3 hours before the Spelling Bee.

But how am I going to remember  **1000 WORDS** in 3 hours?

WEDNESDAY

I retook my Scare exam today.

...And I aced it!

I followed Mr. Matsumoto's advice and I just imagined I was an ugly, scary, hideous human named Big Mouth Jeff. It worked like a charm

It also helped that **THE MINER** I scared was an 8 year old girl.

Hey, as long as she was in the mines, she was fair game. It wasn't my fault it was "Bring Your Daughter to Work Day" for the miners.

"Well done, Zombie-san," Mr. Matsumoto said. "You have a very rare gift."

"You mean my terrifyingly scary miner scaring skills?"

"No, you still have a baby face. But your **ABILITY TO IMAGINE** yourself into becoming scary is very powerful."

"Just remember Zombie-san, if you put your mind to it, you can accomplish anything. You just need to use your imagination."

Wow. Coming from the **10 TIME** Scare champion of the Moblympics, that meant a lot.

I was really happy I passed my Scare exam. But, I still needed to come up with a way to win that Spelling Bee.

I guess I'm just going to have to study and hope that I remember some of the words.

Now, what day is the Spelling Bee again? Uh...

Oh man, I think I'm in trouble...

✳ THURSDAY ✳

I got a list of words to study for the Spelling Bee today.

I'm probably going to forget most of the words by the Spelling Bee tomorrow, but I have to **AT LEAST** give it a try.

Creepy decided to help me out. But he's not the best speller in the world. He still thinks you spell the word Creeper with a 'K.'

I started with the most misspelled words from previous Minecraft Spelling Bees. Words like:

- [x] Obsidian
- [x] Netherrack
- [x] Lapis Lazuli
- [x] Mycelium
- [x] Enchantment
- [x] Cauldron
- [x] Cobblestone
- [x] Podzol
- [x] Prismarine
- [x] Mutton
- [x] Shepherd
- [x] and Pickaxe

I spent the whole day trying to remember these. But, for some reason I kept forgetting them every 3 hours.

I saw Big Mouth Jeff later today. He was bragging again about how he had at least **1000 WORDS** memorized.

1000 Words! How in the world did he do that?

I am so doomed. I'm going to choke and forget all of the words, and I'm going to lose the Spelling Bee. Then I'm going to have to tell everybody that I lied and I don't have a ScareStation 465. And if my parents do buy it for me, I'm going to have to give it to Jeff.

Man, I still don't know how Jeff can memorize so many words. It's like he's using **A MOD TO SPELL** better or something...

Huh?

Wait a minute... No way!

That little... I bet he's cheating!

But how am I going to prove that he is? I mean, I can't just accuse him of cheating in front of everybody. And if he is using a mod, how's he doing it?

I decided to ask the only person I know that ever cheated and got away with it. I went to see Steve.

"Hey Steve, you said you cheated and **GOT AWAY** with it right?"

"Yeah, but don't remind me."

"Well, how did you do it? I mean, how were able to pass your test?"

"Why do you want to know?"

"Well, I think that Big Mouth Jeff is cheating, and that's how he's able to memorize so many words."

"Well, if he is, he's probably using a mod to make his brain **GROW BIGGER.** That's what I did when I passed my exam."

"How did you activate it before your test?"

"I just used an app on my phone. I pulled out my phone before the exam, pushed the button and bam! Bigger brain."

"I bet **THAT'S HOW** Jeff is going to do it too."

"Makes a lot of sense. But how are you going to stop him?"

"Well, I have an idea. But I need your help... You still have that Zombie make up?"

FRIDAY

Well, today is the Spelling Bee.

I almost forgot, but it's a good thing Creepy reminded me.

I did a lot more **STUDYING** last night, but I don't know if any of it stuck or not.

I decided to do some more studying an hour before the Spelling Bee. A lot of the other mob kids were doing the same thing.

We were sitting outside of the auditorium, and Mr. Matsumoto came by.

"Are you ready **TO WIN** your Spelling Bee, Zombie-san?"

"Well, I don't know if I'll win, but I'm going to try my best."

He put his hand on my shoulder and said, "Just remember what I told you, Zombie-san. You can do anything you put your mind to. You just need to use your imagination... No matter **HOW SMALL** you think your brain is."

I just smiled and went back to memorizing my flash cards.

I wanted to write this last entry in my journal before the Spelling Bee because I don't know what's going to happen.

All I do know is that, pea-brain or not, I'm going to give it **EVERYTHING** I've got.

FRIDAY NIGHT

I still can't believe things turned out the way they did at the Spelling Bee.

It was crazy.

Well, there we were, sitting on stage at the start of the Spelling Bee.

THE JUDGE explained all of the instructions. But what stood out to me most was when the judge said that if we missed a word, they would ring a bell and you would be out.

And for some reason that bell looked really, really big.

Now, when things got started, all you could hear were **DINGS** left and right.

Something tells me that the mob kids at school aren't very good spellers.

Then it was Jeff's turn.

"M-Y-C-E-L-I-U-M. Mycelium."

"That is correct."

Then it was my turn.

"N-E-T-H-E-R-R-A-C-K. Netherrack."

"That is correct."

I couldn't believe it. I was doing it!

After the next round, there were more and more dings.

Then it was Jeff's turn again.

"O-B-S-I-D-I-A-N. Obsidian."

"That is correct."

Then it was **MY TURN.**

"C-O-B-B-L-E-S-T-O-N-E. Cobblestone."

"That is correct."

By the end of the second round only Jeff and I were left. They decided to give us a small bathroom break before the last round.

When **THE BREAK** was over, we got back on stage.

As I looked over at Jeff, he still had that smirk on his face like he knew something nobody else did.

But, then I looked toward the back and I could see Steve in his Zombie makeup. He waved a phone at me and gave me a **THUMBS UP.**

"Ok everyone, these are the last words," the judge said. "If only one of you gets their word right, you will be the new Mob Scare School Spelling Bee champion."

Jeff went first.

"Are you ready? The word is Pickaxe."

Jeff smiled at the audience with his **COCKY SMILE,** then he started spelling the word.

"P...Uh..."

"I...Uh..."

"C...Uh..."

"Uh..."

"Can you give the definition, please?"

"A tool miners use to break stones. Pickaxe."

"P...Uh..."

"I...Uh..."

"C...Uh...Uh...Um..."

"A...Uh..."

"X?"

DING!

"That is incorrect."

The whole room gave a big, "Oooohhh."

Then it was my turn.

"Your word is **SHEPHERD.**"

Yes! I studied that word over and over so I wouldn't forget it like I did before. And this time I wasn't going to choke.

"Shepherd"

"S...Uh..."

"H...Uh...Um..."

All of a sudden as I started to spell the word, everything just went **BLANK.** I couldn't remember anything.

I couldn't remember what happened yesterday. I couldn't remember what I did this morning. I couldn't even remember what I did before coming into the auditorium.

"Excuse me, son, the word is Shepherd. You have one minute to answer," the judge said.

All I could hear was the judge's voice, but I couldn't think of anything in my head.

I looked around the whole room and everyone was staring at me. I saw Steve. I saw Sally. I saw Creepy,

Skelee, and Slimey. I even saw Mom and Dad.

But I had nothing.

Then I saw Mr. Matsumoto. And he made a gesture and pointed to his head.

Then I **REMEMBERED** what he said! "You can do anything you put your mind to. You just need to use your imagination."

Then I started imagining that I was a shepherd. I imagined playing with the sheep. I imagined I was Mr. Matsumoto having to master his scaring skills by practicing on pigs and sheep. Then I imagined staring at **THE SHEEP** in the Zombie Farm outside of class. Then I imagined being a big giant, hideous Big

Mouth Jeff humanoid monster. Then I remembered that rush of feeling I felt before and then I yelled out at the top of my voice:

"HYEEEEAAAAAHHHUURRRGHHH-HHZZZOOWWIIIIEEEEE!!!!!"

"Shepherd. S-H-E-P-H-E-R-D. Shepherd!"

"That is correct!"

The whole auditorium blew up in a BIG CHEER.

"And the winner of this year's Mob Scare School Spelling Bee is Mr. Zack Zombie."

I couldn't believe it. I did it.

I looked over at Steve as he walked over to Big Mouth Jeff.

"Here you go, Jeff," Steve said. "I think you dropped this."

After handing Jeff his phone, Steve came over and gave me a high five.

I looked over at Mr. Matsumoto and he gave me a big smile. I smiled back as I pointed to my head.

Then I went back to **CELEBRATE.**

It was the best night ever!

The new Mob Scare School Spelling Bee Champion

SATURDAY

Hey, this is Steve.

I'm writing this for my buddy Zombie who left his journal at the Spelling Bee last night. And I got a few things I want to say...

Well, whoever said that you needed brains to be great at something probably didn't have a Zombie for a friend.

And my friend Zombie is the best friend anybody could have—whether you're a human or if you're a mob.

And the biggest thing that I've learned from hanging out with Zombie these past few weeks is that:

It doesn't matter if you're nervous or scared...

And it doesn't matter if you make a mistake...

And it doesn't matter if you think you're weak or you think you're dumb...

And it doesn't matter if you only have a pea-brain...

Because, as long as you put your mind to it, you can do anything...

All it takes is a little imagination.

...And a few crazy friends that love playing the ScareStation 465!

Ha ha!

Later...

Steve

P.S. By the way Zombie... Looking forward to your birthday party.

FIND OUT WHAT HAPPENS NEXT!

IT'S HALLOWEEN and **Zombie's birthday is coming soon!**

But there's a **ZOMBIE APOCALYPSE** happening that may totally ruin his Birthday party. Will Zombie and his friends be able to **STOP** the Zombie Apocalypse so that they can finally **ENJOY** Zombie's Birthday Bash? Jump into the Next Adventure and Find Out!

Made in the USA
Coppell, TX
29 February 2020

16374065R00108